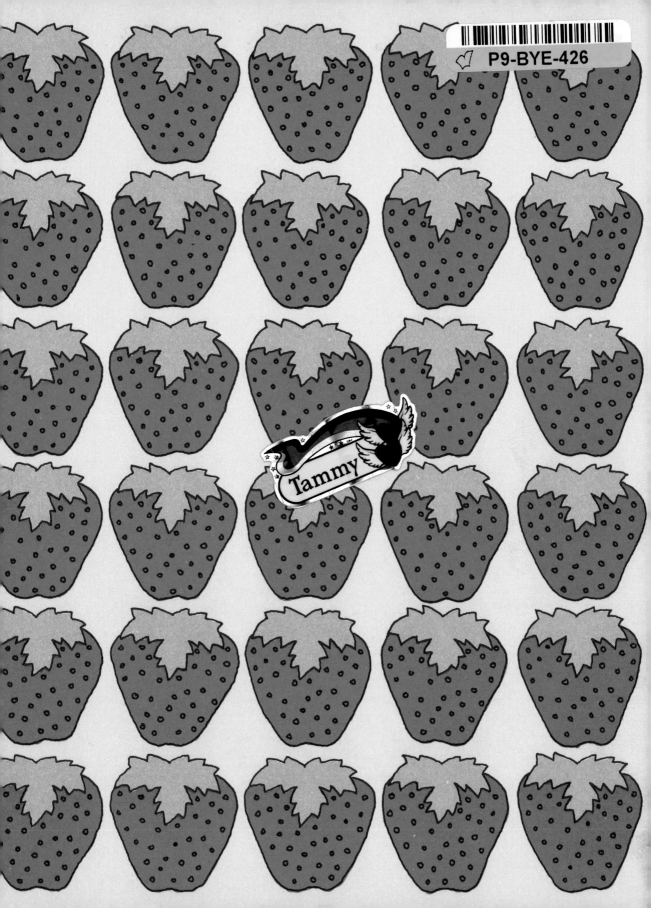

Tammy

THE STICKYBEAR FAMILY ™

Bedford Stickybear   **Sara Stickybear**

Bumper Stickybear

this
strawberry library
of first learning
book
belongs to

Printed in the United States of America.

Stickybear™ is the registered trademark of Optimum Resource, Inc.
Strawberry® and A Strawberry Book® are the registered
trademarks of One Strawberry, Inc.

Weekly Reader Books' Edition

Library of Congress Cataloging in Publication Data

Hefter, Richard.
   Neat feet.

   (Stickybear books)
   Summary: The antics of the Stickybears illustrate the
concepts: in, out, up, down, over, under, in front of, and
behind.
      1. English language – Prepositions – Juvenile litera-
ture.   [1. English language – Prepositions.   2. Vocab-
ulary]   I. Title   II. Series: Hefter, Richard.
Stickybear books.
PE1335.H43   1983   425   83-8035
ISBN 0-911787-07-0

neat
feet

by Richard Hefter

Optimum Resource, Inc. • Connecticut

Bears behind boxes.

Bears in boxes.

Bears on boxes.

Bears under boxes.

Boxes.

Bears.

Bears in front of
broken boxes.

Bears go up.

Bears come down.

Bears are standing upside down.

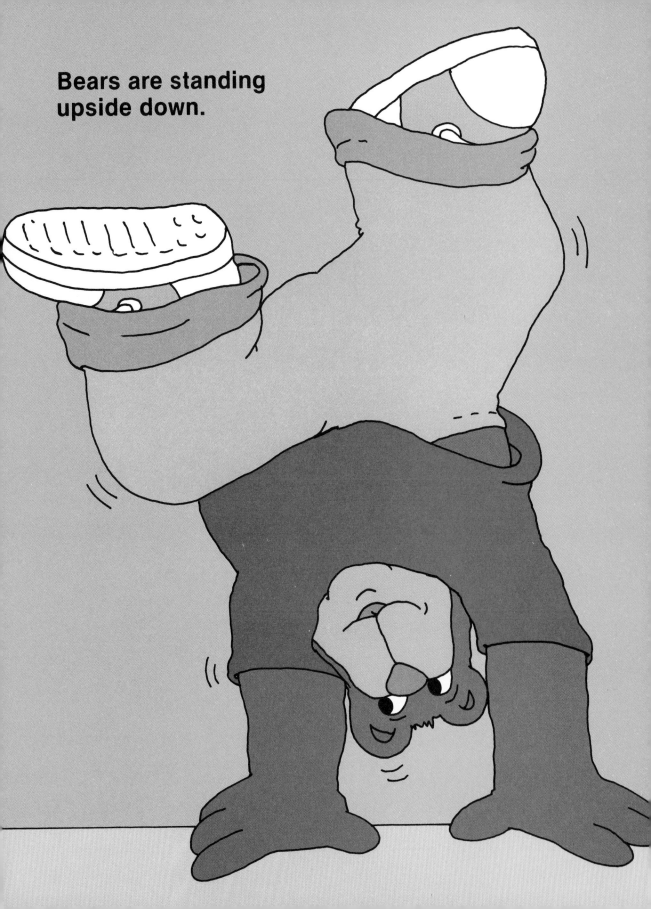

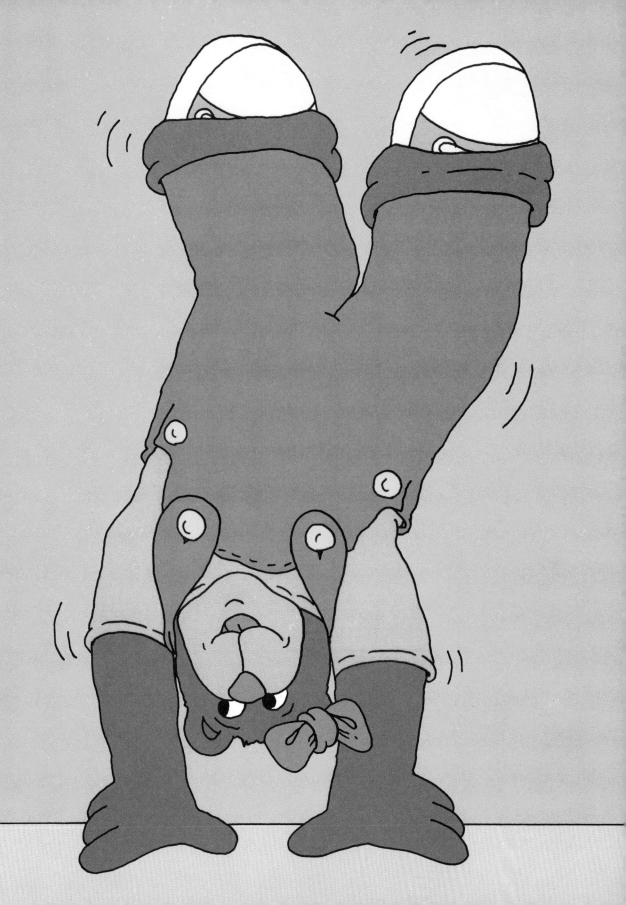

Bears go in.

Bears come out.

Bears kick up their feet
and shout.

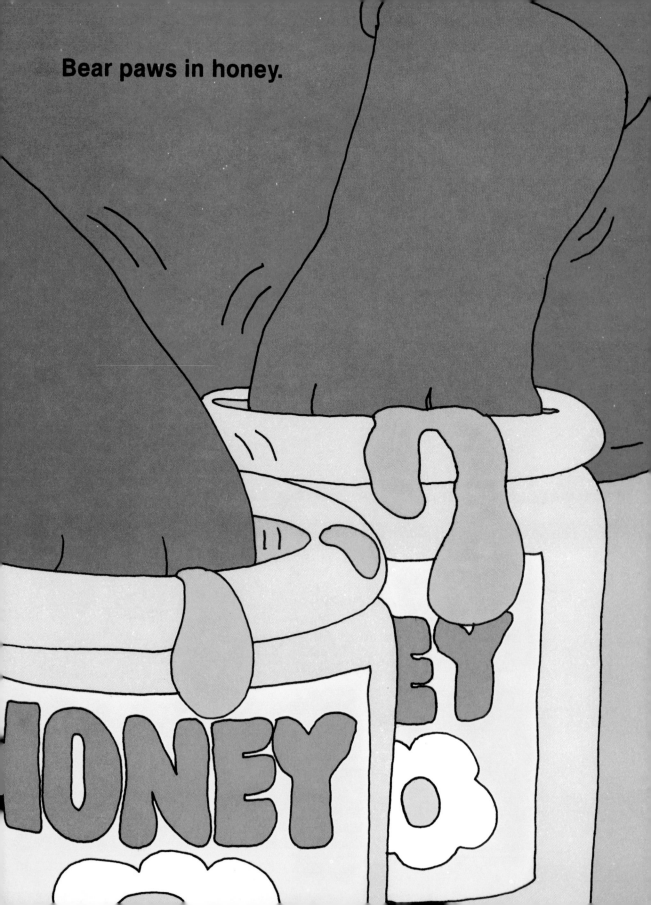

Bear paws in honey.

Honey on bears.

Sweet, sticky bears.

Neat feet.

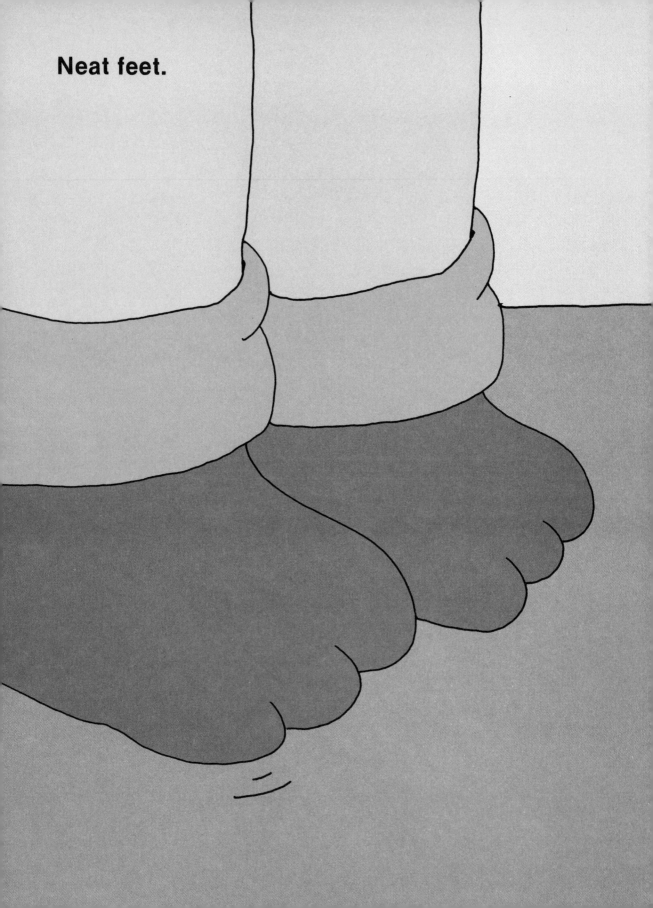

Blue socks.

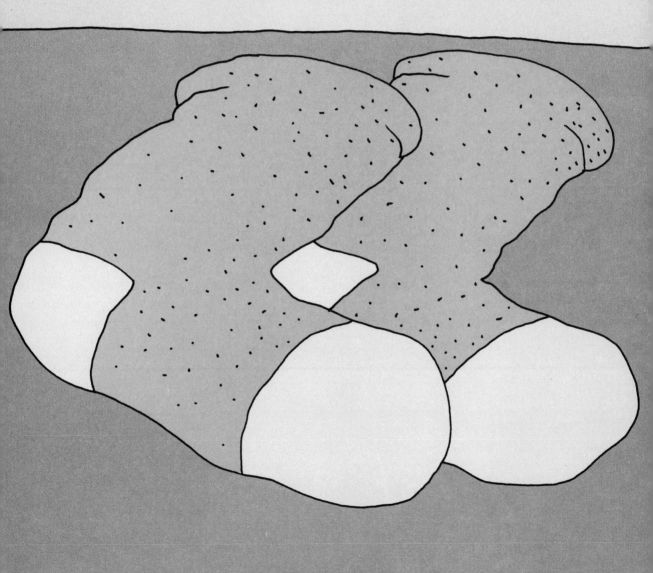

Neat feet in blue socks
jumping over lumpy rocks.

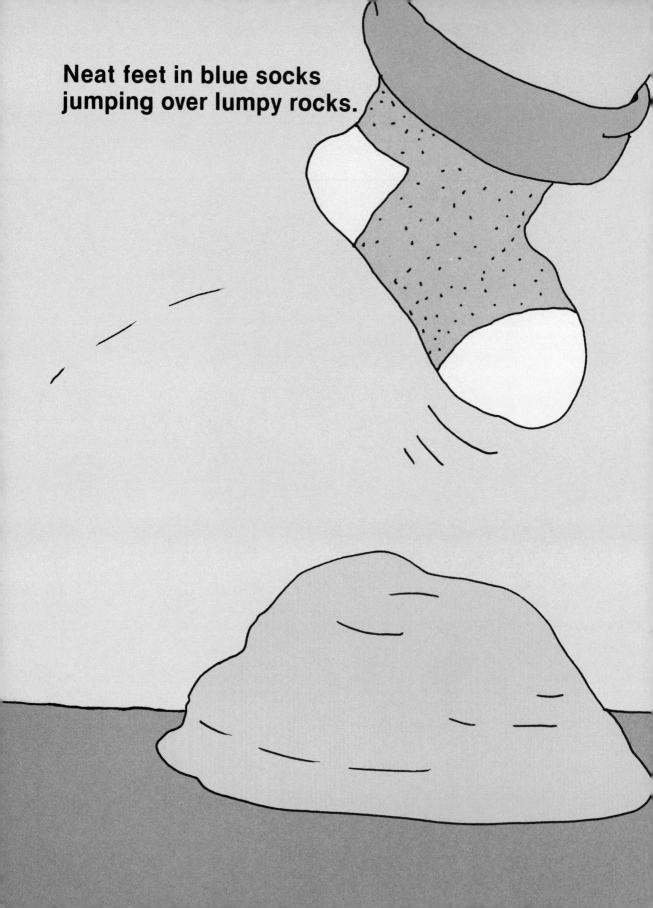

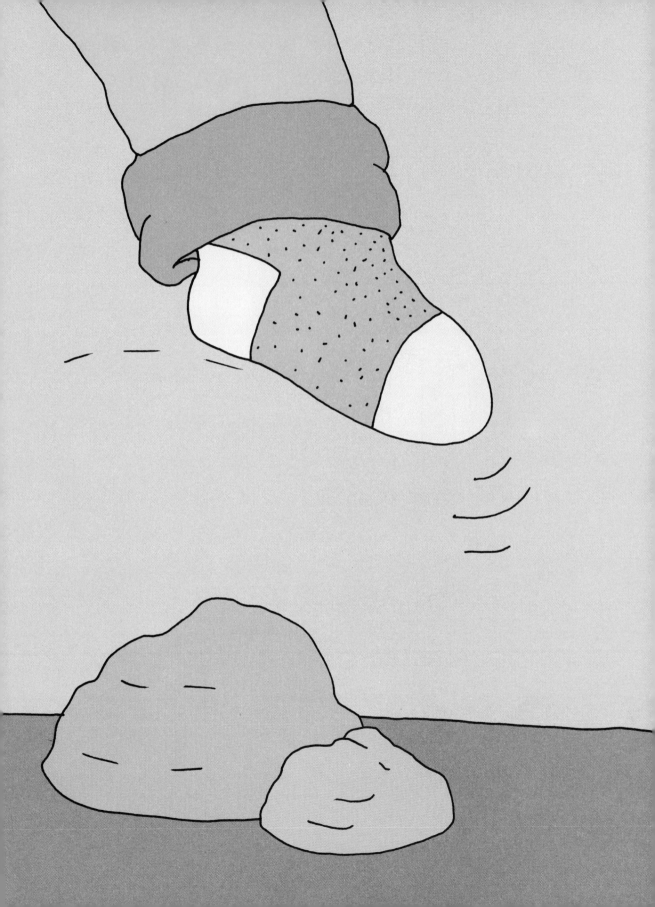

Bears crawling under chairs.
Bears jumping over chairs.

Tired bears.

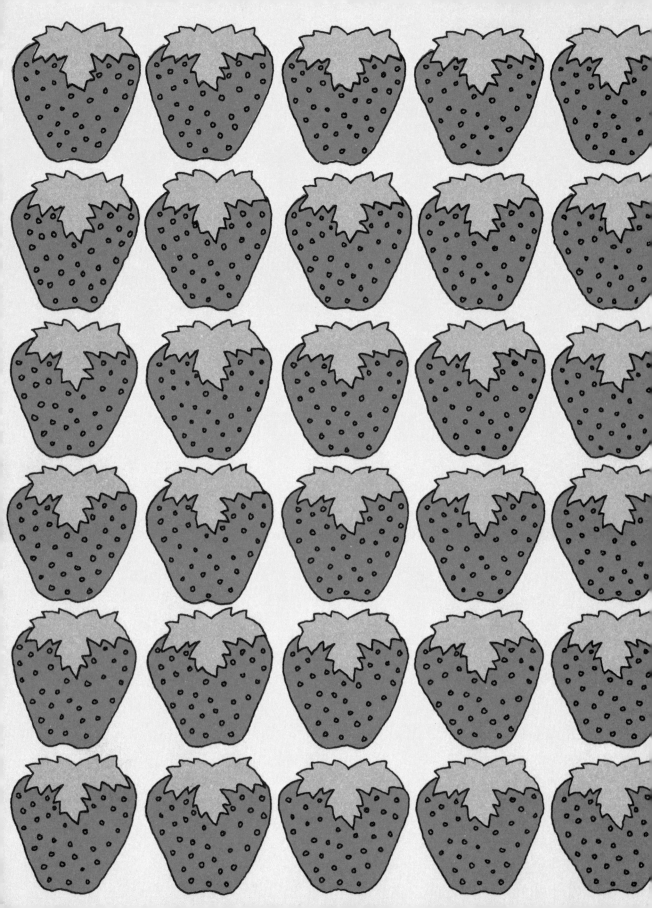